my big

sister

by Valorie Fisher

Atheneum Books for Young Readers

New York London Toronto Sydney Singapore

ACKNOWLEDGMENTS

I am immensely grateful to Elinor Hills for her hard work, gracious smile, and delightful scowl. I would like to thank my son, Aidan, for being the perfect photographer's assistant and for lending me Bullet, Brooklyn's fastest goldfish; Bernadette Frishberg, a most expressive baby; Isadora and Miles Schappell-Spillman, whose Frances Popcorn was a lovely guinea pig of enormous talent; my mother, Susan Fisher, a rodent milliner extraordinaire; Mia and Romy Faucher-Mayhew for their much-too-much-loved dolls; and my brother, Kevin Fisher, for his insight into sisters, big and little. And I am deeply grateful for the continued support, enthusiasm, and friendship of Lee Wade and Anne Schwartz.

Atheneum Books for Young Readers

An imprint of Simon & Schuster Children's Publishing Division

1230 Avenue of the Americas

New York, New York 10020

Book design by Lee Wade

The text for this book is set in Filosophia.

Manufactured in China

2 4 6 8 10 9 7 5 3 1

Library of Congress Cataloging-in-Publication Data

Fisher, Valorie.

My big sister / Valorie Fisher.

p. cm.

Summary: Photographs and simple text illustrate

baby's view of what it is like to have a big sister.

ISBN-13: 978-1-4169-3544-5

ISBN-10: 1-4169-3544-4

[1. Sisters—Fiction. 2. Babies—Fiction.] I. Title.

PZ7.F53485 Mye 2004

[E]—dc21

2002006732

For Mom and Dad

This is my
big sister.

It's hard for me to keep up with her.

She takes very good care of me,

except when
she leaves me
with the neighbor.

She likes to pick out everyone's clothes.

My big sister
kisses me,

and sometimes
she doesn't.

If I'm good,
she takes me
to the zoo

or introduces me
to her friends.

But I'm not supposed to bother her when she's working.

Animal training takes up a lot of her time.

My big sister
gets oodles of
phone calls;

sometimes she
lets me talk too.

I love my
big sister,

and she loves me.

Attach photo here.

Attach photo here.

my big sister

me

To preserve your pictures keep an acid and lignin free tissue sheet over them when the book is closed.